*There are many versions of this classic
tale. In the tradition of the storyteller,
each one is uniquely different.*

Library of Congress Cataloging-in-Publication Data

José, Eduard.
  Aladdin's lamp.

  (A Classic tale)
  Translation of: Aladino y la lampara
maravillosa.
  At head of title: From "The Arabian nights."
  Summary: Recounts the tale of a poor boy who
becomes a wealthy prince with the help of a magic
lamp he finds in an enchanted cave.
  [1. Fairy tales. 2. Folklore, Arab]
  I. Lavarello, José M., ill. II. Suire, Diane Dow,
1954-   . III. Aladdin. IV. Title.
  V. Series.
PZ8.J747Al 1988   398.2'1   [E]   88-35312
ISBN 0-89565-481-4

© 1988 Parramón Ediciones, S.A.
Printed in Spain by Sirven Gràfic, S.A.
© Alexander Publishers' Marketing
and The Child's World, Inc.: English
edition, 1988.
L.D.: B-44.044-88

FROM "THE ARABIAN NIGHTS"

Aladdin's Lamp

Illustration: José M. Lavarello
Adaptation: Eduard José

Retold by Diane Suire

The Child's World, Inc.

Long ago, in a great city far away, there lived a boy named Aladdin. Aladdin's father had died when the boy was very young, and his mother worked hard, spinning cotton to buy the food she and her son needed.

One day, a stranger came to Aladdin's house claiming to be his uncle. Now, this stranger was not really Aladdin's uncle at all—he was a magician. And he had a plan up his sleeve.

"Come with me," the magician told Aladdin. "If you do what I say, you will soon be very rich."

Because Aladdin and his mother were so poor, the magician's offer sounded wonderful.

And so, the next day, Aladdin went outside the town with the magician. Suddenly, the old man stopped. He cleared away the sand to reveal a big stone with a brass ring fixed in its top.

"Take hold of the ring," said the magician. "Lift up the top." Beneath the stone were some steps leading downward.

"Follow the steps," said the magician. "They lead to a room filled with treasures. Do not touch anything you see except for a lamp standing on marble. Bring the lamp to me. If you do as I say, I'll make you rich. And here, take this ring. It will protect you."

Aladdin took the ring and went down the stairs. There he entered a room where his eyes were dazzled by all that he saw.

Finding the lamp surrounded by treasures, Aladdin picked it up and headed for the staircase. At the top of the stairs, the magician was waiting for him.

"Give me the lamp," the magician ordered.

But Aladdin did not completely trust his so-called uncle, who somehow seemed evil. Aladdin feared that the man would grab the lamp and then drop the stone door over the staircase. So Aladdin said, "Help me out, and then I'll give you the lamp."

Now the magician was furious. He had read in his magic books that the lamp could make him the most powerful man in the world—but only if it were given to him by the hand of another. Now the boy was ruining everything! In a fit of rage, the magician shouted some magic words and sealed the entrance with a burst of flame. Then, since his plan was ruined, he returned to Africa, from where he had come.

Aladdin was left in complete darkness. In his grief, he rubbed the lamp against his chest. Instantly, a huge genie appeared.

"I am your slave, my lord and master! Command and I obey," the genie said.

Amazed, Aladdin asked to be taken home. In the twinkling of an eye it was done!

Aladdin told his mother all about what had happened. They decided to keep the lamp a secret. They thought that if they used it just once in awhile, no one would suspect anything. And so the years passed happily for Aladdin and his mother. When they needed food or clothes, they asked the genie. If they needed money to pay taxes to the king, they asked the genie.

Then one day Aladdin's life changed completely. He saw the face of the king's daughter as she was going to the public baths. Although it was forbidden to look at the princess, Aladdin could not help himself. The moment he saw the princess, he fell in love with her and wanted to marry her.

Moved by his great love, Aladdin dressed in his best clothes. He asked the genie to gather a small chest full of the most wonderful jewels that had ever been seen on earth.

After waiting several days, Aladdin was granted permission to see the king. Opening the chest of jewels, he knelt before the king.

"Your Majesty," he said, "I know that my request is great. But I love your daughter and want to marry her. As proof of my love, I have brought this small gift."

The king was astonished! The shining jewels sparkled. "How beautiful!" he exclaimed.

The king was very excited by the thought of having such a wealthy son-in-law. But before he agreed to let his daughter marry Aladdin, he wanted to see just how rich and powerful this young man was. So he said, "Build a castle for my daughter. Then I will grant the wedding."

As soon as Aladdin was alone, he again summoned the genie and asked him to build the finest castle imaginable next to the king's palace. No sooner said than done—the castle appeared instantly.

Flabbergasted by this display of power, the king not only granted Aladdin his daughter's hand, but the wedding took place that very day.

The kingdom hummed with excitement. Everyone was happy about the wedding. That is, everyone but the grand vizier, who had hoped to marry the princess himself. Now that his hopes were dashed, the grand vizier was furious. He ordered his spies to discover the secret of Aladdin's power.

When he learned from them that the young man's entire fortune came from the magic lamp, the vizier disguised himself as a beggar. He bought several lamps and went near the palace calling, "New lamps for old! I'll change your old lamps for new ones."

As fate would have it, the princess remembered having seen her husband's lamp in a corner of a closet. With no idea of the harm she could do, she made the trade while Aladdin was away hunting.

As soon as the lamp was in the vizier's hands, he rubbed it. In an instant, the huge genie appeared. The vizier commanded that the castle, the princess, and he himself be carried far, far away. And so it was.

Then the evil vizier set to work trying to convince the princess to marry him and forget about Aladdin. "You will never see Aladdin again," said the vizier. "He is as good as dead."

Of course, when Aladdin came home, he was full of grief. He ran about the city asking everyone what had become of his castle and wife. But the people only shook their heads. They didn't know. Aladdin was in deep despair.

Then, suddenly, Aladdin remembered the magic ring that the evil magician had given him many years ago. He quickly rubbed the ring and the genie of the ring magically appeared.

"Oh, Genie!" said Aladdin. "You must help me! Bring back my wife and castle at once!"

"I am sorry, Master," said the genie of the ring. "But I do not have the power to do that. Only the genie of the lamp can bring them back. But I can take you to your wife."

"Yes, yes! Hurry!" said Aladdin. And before he could blink, Aladdin was in the castle.

"My husband," cried the princess, running to him.

When Aladdin learned of the exchange of the lamps, he knew he must get the magic lamp back.

"I have a plan," said Aladdin to the princess. "Here is some sleeping powder. Now you must do exactly as I tell you to do." He told her the whole plan and then hid behind a curtain.

When the vizier came home, the princess told him she was ready to marry him. "I realize that I can't avoid my fate. Let us drink to our happiness."

As she said this, she gave the vizier a glass of wine containing the sleeping powder. The wicked man drank the wine and fell fast asleep.

Then Aladdin came out of hiding. Quickly, he took the magic lamp which hung from the vizier's waist and rubbed it. In a flash, the genie of the lamp appeared, and Aladdin asked that the castle be moved back to where it had been.

Instantly, his wish was granted. At that moment, the king happened to be looking out a window of his palace. He was amazed by the wondrous sight. Soon, the princess and her father were in one another's arms. And the vizier was sent to prison.

Months later, the king proclaimed Aladdin his heir and successor. "I feel sure," said the king, "that after I die, you will rule the kingdom honestly and fairly."

As for the magic lamp, it was left in a drawer in the royal chamber. Aladdin never needed it again. The happiness he felt with his wife and the children that came was greater than any fortune that magic could bestow upon him.